Northwestern Mutual®

Skacky – Adventures in Imagination is sponsored by Nick Wallace and Wallace Financial, in partnership with Northwestern Mutual.

Wallace Financial is a financial planning practice that works with parents across the United States, specifically in planning for the future of a child with disabilities.

Web: www.nickwallace.nm.com
Email: nick.wallace@nm.com
Phone: 859-302-1223

For Jordan

Timothy A. Pack, *author/illustrator*

\# __73__ of a series of 300

Skacky

Adventures in Imagination

Timothy A. Pack

JOEY BOOKS
Morley, Missouri

 *An imprint of* **Acclaim Press™** — *Your Next Great Book* —

P.O. Box 238
Morley, MO 63767
(573) 472-9800
www.acclaimpress.com

Author: Timothy A. Pack

ISBN: 978-1-956027-19-8 | 1-956027-19-X
Library of Congress Control Number: 2022930159

First Printing: 2022
Printed in the United States of America
10 9 8 7 6 5 4 3 2 1

This book is dedicated to my son Josiah, whose imagination breathed life into his favorite toys.
In choosing, naming, and animating his toys, an otherwise silent child found his voice.
In a creative expression of caring, adventure, humor, and love, Josiah gives us a
window into autism, and shows us the value of belonging.

This story is the product of Josiah's childhood imagination. He gave these toys their names and personalities. He animated them the way any child does when playing.

Yet for the parent of an unusual and silent child, it opened up joyous vistas for anxious parents. This is a story of relationship. Though other characters are mentioned—with their various traits and personalities—the story is really about this one relationship—Josiah and Skacky.

Skacky is chosen. He is given a name. He is given a voice and a personality. He is given an identity. He is given a community. He is given adventure—including danger—and at last he is given special status, even regal station! Josiah's decision to do all this flows from his love. By contrast, the others in Josiah's room who did not receive such attention, were either bit players, or essentially dead by comparison.

All of this should sound familiar to the Christian reader, who may claim the very same wondrous privilege from having been treated likewise by the One Who chose us!

Similarly, the parent of an autistic child can have unique fears, and doubts, and apprehension for what they do not know nor understand about their child. The opportunity to appreciate the interactions of their mysterious child with beloved things, can unlock a lot of those mysteries.

I don't know how I got here,
but I have learned my name.
And I can tell a story 'bout
what's happened since I came.

See, there's a boy who lives here.
He chose me long ago,
to live among my other friends.
His Mommy calls him Jo.

My name is Skacky, that one's Wil. That's Zing, Pierre, and Jess. Here's Bo-Bo, George, and Ellie too. Gosh,...this place is a mess!

Jesse is a watchful eye,
to look out for the cat.

Annie is an octopus,
who sings, and stuff like that.

Bo-Bo is a monkey
who thinks that he is not.

Pierre is a penguin
who goes "Oui, oui" a lot.

Zing is always going fast!
Watch out, he's
coming through!

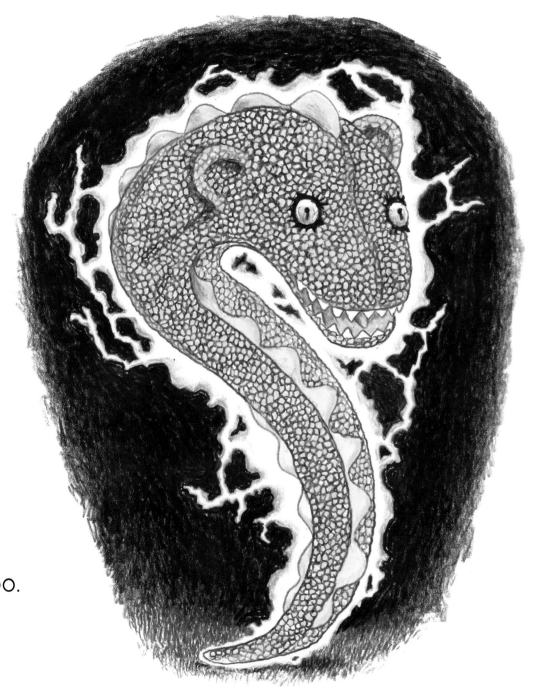

Ellie's an electric eel
who's very friendly too.

Wilbear is a giant,
but he really isn't mean.

George is not the smartest,
but knows words like
"book" and "bean."

The things that happen 'round here are dull most of my days.
But danger lurks beyond the bed. At least that's what *they* say.

Sure, I've fallen from some places–like top shelves of the rack.

It's scary falling through the air, but I always bounce right back!

And I've been left out in the floor before Jo goes to bed.
If I was made of weaker stuff I'd prob'ly wake up dead!

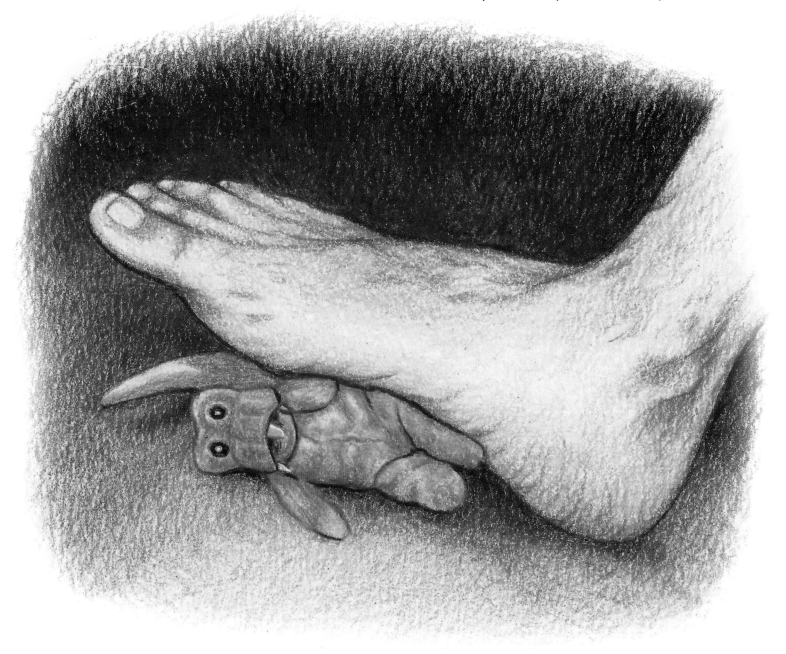

And Dusty is a dangerous cat.
She slaps me like a toy.
And though I don't much care for
that, it's funny to the boys.

I get to go with little Jo and watch him brush his teeth.
Then sit beside his comforter, and watch my best friend sleep.

He talks to me and I talk too
whenever we are near. And even
though I have no mouth,
I speak and Jo Jo hears.

21

What am I supposed to be? Some say a crocodile.
A dinosaur? A lizard? Or a dragon with a smile?

I used to be a brighter green.
My hide was not so worn.
But love has scuffed me up a bit,
since my best pal was born.

My only world is in this house,
another one's out there.
I saw it on a bike ride once –
it gave me quite a scare!

I even rode a big jet plane! To where? I can't recall.
The world below, to me, so large, up there became so small!

There's other things here in the room
that never make a sound. They have no life,
they never move when Jo Jo is around.

The toys that
mean the most to
Jo are others in
the floor,
and scattered
'cross the
dresser top, and
over by the door.

The soldiers, and the
figures, whose actions
Jo commands;
the dog-eared books,
the tattered ship,...and
stuffed toy in his hand.

What makes me live
when others don't?
What makes this toy a king?

It's love that brings
my heart to life, his voice
that makes me sing!

Author's Statement

According to the **Center for Autism Spectrum Disorders**, 1 in 54 children in the U.S. are affected by autism. For many parents, the discovery that their child is on the autism spectrum can be devastating. Parents can come away from their child's diagnosis feeling overwhelmed. There are often so many concerns and questions.

Such was the case for the Pack family in 2003. Josiah, the fifth son of Timothy and Joyce Pack, was diagnosed with what was then called *Asperger's Syndrome*. Josiah was silent. He was developmentally delayed. He was "different." Well-meaning friends and acquaintances would sometimes ask, "what will become of Josiah?"

This book, *Skacky: Adventures in Imagination*, is the beginning of an answer to that troubling question. This charming story is narrated by Josiah's favorite stuffed animal. Josiah's vivid imagination, creativity, and sense of humor animated his toys in a delightful way that opened a window into Jo's world. An otherwise silent child communicated volumes through his relationship with Skacky.

In many ways the character Skacky represents Josiah himself. He is chosen and loved. He is given a name, a community, an identity and purpose. He is given adventure, privilege, and even an exalted status. Josiah thrived in all this love, even as his little friend did.

Families embark on an "Autism Adventure" with their child. It seems daunting. They have a diagnosis, a stack of papers, facts and figures, and an unclear future. And yet,… they also have a wondrous child to love! This child's "malady" can, in time, be seen as a "super-power." There are mysteries to be discovered. Timothy Pack hopes that *Skacky: Adventures in Imagination* will encourage families like his own—that the love they have for their child will provide a fun, creative, living world of promising possibilities.

— *Timothy Pack*

About the Author

Timothy Pack is an illustrator, artist, and writer who lives in Lexington, Kentucky with his wife of 40 years. They have four adult sons and five grandchildren. Pack's family and life experience in pastoral care and missionary chaplaincy have continually inspired his art, poetry, and songs.